THE WAR OF PERSPECTIVES

Break the Rule to Make a New One

Vivekanand Jha

ISBN 979-8-89186-437-5

<u>(4-5-1952 to 15-9-2023)</u>

I wanted to dedicate this book to my dear father, late Prof. Shri Bhogendra Jha, a great teacher, an inspiring mentor, a brilliant thought leader, an admirable social worker and above all an excellent human soul. He used to say, *'The only way to live your life is to pursue happiness. Do what you like and be happy with smile on your face in all the situations you encounter in your life. And he used to practice it in his day to day life. He was very clear in his thought process and took his decision accordingly, taking risk more than his capacity and practice to survive in odd situations. His perspectives of life was to "create happiness around you to be happy", and always help others generously who need your help, he always carry larger perspective of life understanding there is an end to it. He always admire of his knowledge about village of India and agriculture. He used to see village of India as an independent source of growth and prosperity for India.*

CONTENTS

PREFACE

Dear reader,

It is with great anticipation and enthusiasm that I embark on the challenge of articulating my individual, social, and environmental perspectives. I have always believed that a supernatural power gives us strength and guides us, with help of multiple honest efforts by people, towards the place where we need to be. I say 'multiple efforts' because achieving success on the first attempt may lead to missed opportunities for innovation and growth. When we succeed right away without encountering challenges, we might not gain the necessary experience or understanding to add new perspectives and use cases to our knowledge. I firmly believe in failure being a part of innovation and success.

My journey was a journey from a small village primary school to a big B-school, from being a small village boy to a big corporate employee, and from a slow-growing India to a fast-growing India (before and after 1991 respectively). The true measurement of the current Indian society can be gauged by considering the periods before and after the Indian market opened up for the world in 1991. This landmark event, known as economic liberalisation or 'LPG' (Liberalisation, Privatisation, and Globalisation), marked a significant turning point in India's economic policies and its integration into the global economy.

In penning this book, I aspired to connect with millions of individuals from diverse backgrounds—whether they are from rural or urban areas/metropolises, whether millennials or high-ranking executives. Being rooted in a small village endows us with immense fortitude and opens doors to grandeur at any level, in any place, and under any circumstance. It also equips us with life skills essential for thriving in any situation.

When we start our journey, we are open to accepting any challenge and grabbing opportunities. We can't solve our problems by being big—

we start adding limitations with each step of success. If we want to analyse the world of success, we have only two methods at our disposal: either we belong to a less privileged section of society, which allows us to gain first-hand experience, or we go to the lowest level and move up each step theoretically to understand the journey to the top.

It may take multiple attributes for us to define our journey, but I feel changes in communication with experience are the keys to success. Clarity of thought improves with each step of experience. When we are at the lowest rung, communication is very difficult, and there we learn about the perspectives of people, society, and environments at a more granular level. Imagine, at a younger age, when we learn more, our effective communication skills are almost non-existent. With experience, our effective communication gets sharper and indeed becomes result-oriented. Fundamentally, no one practises effective communication, but when you grow, your communication and engagement become effective and learning perspectives makes it easier to execute results or deliverables.

While in the realm of books and theories, we may think we know everything, but when we start working in an organisation, things often don't go as planned. This is where the '25% genetic and 75% environmental impact' physiological principle comes into play. The genetic aspect represents the way we learn theoretical knowledge gained through studies, while the environmental impact indicates the significance of interpersonal skills developed through social engagement and experiences in various social environments. Even within the 75% environmental impact involves learning about multiple technologies, tools, techniques, and case studies to enhance the quality of our work. However, it is often through failures that we truly understand the perspectives of both sides.

Perspective is intricate and emerges from a combination of three key elements: human environment, behaviour, and actions. The fusion of action and environmental data points gives us insights into the behaviour of any individual, the environment they operate in, and the society they belong to.

In the course of my corporate journey, I have come to define the current era of corporate lifestyle in a single sentence: 'Nothing matters in corporate life if we are meeting the perspectives of others until we become powerful.' In this fast-paced corporate world, personal life is a precious gift bestowed upon us by a supernatural power and each moment must be cherished and valued.

I realised how important it is to align one's journey in the right manner if one is to navigate the rapidly growing world and build a better world with great satisfaction. Understanding the perspectives of those around us becomes the core attribute for survival in this world. Indeed, the post 1991 generation in India has experienced significant turbulence and this impact is seen across South East Asian societies and the world. Things that once mattered the most in our lives can quickly become irrelevant after some time due to the rapid pace of change and technological advancements. We have witnessed an astonishing speed in adopting the latest technologies and products, often skipping over some very famous technologies from developed nations that were no more relevant for developing countries.

This fast pace of change and the adaptation of new technologies and products have both positive and negative consequences. On the one hand, they enhance our experiences and improve our lives in many ways. On the other hand, it can sometimes feel like **well-marketed products or technologies are trap, leading us into cycles of constant upgrades, without our fully understanding how to use most of them or if it is really required.** Let's take a few examples to illustrate this phenomenon:

- Maruti 800, once considered a social status symbol, became outdated after the market opened up in 1991. Newer car models flooded the Indian automobile industry. The car become an economically viable option.

- The transition from reel and digital cameras to mobile phones with built-in cameras around the early 2000s made standalone cameras less popular.

- Data storage technologies have evolved rapidly, from floppy disks to CD drives, and then to pen drives and hard disk drives. Now, with cloud computing, we carry our entire digital world in virtual storage.

- The evolution of internet connectivity has been remarkable, moving from wired connections cable to faster fibre-optic networks and now wireless Wi-Fi technologies.

- In terms of income, what was once considered a big deal, like a monthly salary of INR 3,500 in India, has become insignificant compared to salaries reaching Lacs today.

These examples highlight how our lives have been shaped by constant change and adaptation, leading to both progress and challenges. As a generation, we have witnessed an incredible transformation, and it's crucial to remain adaptable and open-minded to make the most of the opportunities and tackle the complexities of this rapidly evolving world.

Nothing impossible, what truly matters is maintaining a 360-degree thought process and meeting your perspective, aligning your long-term goal and social responsibilities so that everyone has 'life skills' and access to -quality food and good health. This gives us the perspective that nothing matters and proves the universal law of change, i.e. that change is the only sustainable phenomenon. Never think of feeling low/depressed in any situation. Please don't hesitate to accept changes at any point of time.

I started to pen down thoughts with case studies to understand the concept of perspective in the right manner, not as per data or data analytics, which wipe out the behaviour of others or focus on changing others' behaviour as per business needs or the business perspective. And when we are a developing nation, our perspective changes with time. And we understand others' perspectives, which arise from the need to be in the system or relevant to their time. And we need to align ourselves with changing targets or organisational perspectives at the same speed. When we work with multiple perspectives simultaneously, most of the old, successful case studies or experiences lose their validity, as they are affected by changes in the environmental perspective. Therefore, carrying the baggage of old successful results doesn't work for new innovations.

Failure gives us the next level of life experience. It is also the next level of challenge—the challenge being to not fail the next time. We have to choose between a zero or a one to get a better result from a complex perspective. If we are not making it or failing it then we are only delaying it, and that is a waste of resources and time, which is precious. **We need to understand that failure can be measured but success can't, because we hit a roadblock after success.**

We must embark on our journeys with redefined perspectives that align with the organisation's objectives, regardless of the task at hand. However, it is crucial to validate our perspectives with the organisation's viewpoint to ensure that our outputs meet their optimal needs. So, there is a solution that lies in a newer perspective. It may not be the best-suited solution for an organisation but it evolves a fresh idea that allows the problem to be approached differently, which is satisfying at the level of innovation. **As I mentioned earlier, every part of our life perspective changes with time. So, nothing is right or wrong if we are in a position of control. This means we must experiment with changing perspectives to transform people, relationships, and society according to larger and more long-term positive goals.**

In the current era, all innovations or products backfire against the environment, like mobiles, TVs, computers, ACs, fridges, cars, etc. Every product has a life and there is no definedend-to-end recycling process built into the development and deployment of these products to grow or sustain our businessin the long term. Satellites are undoubtedly among the finest space inventions, providing crucial support for human life. However, approvals for lakhs of satellite launches are currently pending at the international regulatory level, as satellites also have an impact on the earth's atmospheric layer and potentially cause damage to our environment. I am not an expert on every innovation or development but launching so many satellites may have a big impact on our atmospheric layer.

My intent isn't to oppose innovation, but rather to advocate a thorough and honest analysis of their long-term, 360-degree impact to safeguard lives, society, and the environment. Nature has bestowed us with a beautiful Earth that has endured for eons (harking back to the Vedic Yug) and is equipped with all the features we require for our livelihoods. Hence, we must scrutinise the smallest impacts on our innovations have on the Earth. Why should their lifespan be limited to 2 to 10 years? As socially responsible intellectuals, our innovations should prioritise saving lives, not just streamlining activities. Regardless of the challenges that arise, we must dedicate extra effort to simulate, diversify, challenge, and thoroughly analyse products before implementation. Adopt a design thinking approach, create a tangible model, and always consider the smallest impacts on the environment and the lives of people. Always contemplate the impact and long-term perspective of innovations.

The impact of any solution to a problem is directly proportional to its impact on life, health, and the environment. When we seek to tackle challenges or address issues, it is of paramount importance to weigh the potential consequences on these vital aspects.

- ♦ Impact on Life: The solution should strive to bring about positive improvements in people's lives. Whether it involves addressing social, healthcare, or economic issues, the ultimate aim should be to uplift and enhance the quality of life for individuals and communities.

♦ Impact on Health: Health stands as a cornerstone, and any solution must prioritise the well-being of individuals. Whether it entails advancing medical technologies, advocating healthy habits, or addressing environmental factors affecting health, the objective should always be to safeguard and enhance overall well-being.

♦ Impact on the Environment: Environmental sustainability is crucial for the enduring survival of our planet and all its inhabitants. Solutions to problems should be mindful of their ecological footprint and strive to minimise adverse impacts on the environment. Encouraging eco-friendly practices and adhering to the principles of the circular economy can contribute to a healthier planet.

The positive impact of products and services will survive longer than the negative impact, which will not support the organisational perspective in any case. Zooming IN and zooming OUT will give us the actual perspective of the impact of our development. If you think your innovation, development, or change has a very small impact, please zoom IN, and if you think it will break all the records of innovation, please zoom OUT. The same principle allows businesses to survive in the long term with the right innovations.

Our modest endeavour aims to align people, innovations, and growth with the right perspective towards life, health, and the environment. If nothing matters, if nothing is wrong or right, then why set loads of targets and build pressure to innovateand develop new things for human life without the right and long-term perspective? Considering everyone's perspective, we need to add more to create a perfect model of any problem or requirement. **We are human and we are born to perform activities and make some mistakes. The human life cycle revolves around these two parameters—activities and mistakes. And learning is a byproduct of these two actions.** Whether we choose it or not, it shows in our perspectives. However, that doesn't mean we should perform the wrong activity repeatedly and impact human lives. We need to be cautious while performing any activity or advocating any development innovation. It should have a positive impact on lives, the environment and society.

The entire ecosystem functions harmoniously, and in the grand scheme of things, the intricacies of time—past, present, and future—hold little weight when compared to the impact of misguided innovation. Nothing matters before, after and now. As human beings, we are working/innovating/developing to survive, so we need to work for life humanity and avoid the negative impacts of innovations. Please face straight the 'war of perspectives' and think differently from outside to go the extra mile. Long-term growth and revenue will follow.

This book is dedicated to the next generation of working professionals who can take charge of creating the perfect model by adding all the perspectives at the right times, in the right places, and in the right direction—for the betterment of our lives, society, and environment and of humanity as a whole. This book is all about the human perspective, human behaviour, and human action. While working, it is difficult to take a break to reflect, to pause and think about the next step. So, this book is dedicated to final-year students who are preparing for fast growth, fast-changing targets, and fast-moving perspectives in corporate working environments. Let's experience a few hard truths before starting the roller-coaster journey of the business world.

1. PERSPECTIVE

Perspective is a critical parameter that defines the end goal for individuals, societies, and organisations. In today's era, goals and targets have evolved into perspectives, and it is reflected in our behaviour and actions. Thus, a proper understanding of perspective is crucial. Perspective reflects the awareness, depth of knowledge, and behaviour of individuals, society, and the environment. Perspectives have stood the test of time in our society, yielding steady outcomes and contributing to stable social lives. They serve as tools with which to engage in self-calculated behaviour within the human mind, ultimately influencing our actions. The strength of a perspective can fluctuate based on our level of awareness, the information available to us, and the individuals we benchmark ourselves against. Perspective, as the underlying behaviour of humans, has remained a corner stone of every society throughout history. Perspectives of world leaders derived the society multiple times in history. It has been employed and adapted to the needs of the time by intellectuals to steer societies, environments, and individuals. Nevertheless, it is essential to acknowledge that perspectives can have both positive and negative impacts on the society, the environment, and the individuals.

Perspective can be delineated by two parameters: the follower behaviour perspective and the leader behaviour perspective.

- ♦ Follower behaviour perspective: This perspective encompasses the majority of our society, accounting for over 90% of individuals. Follower behaviour perspective is an inherent trait in humans. Our perspectives are moulded by what we witness, observe, and undergo. Our minds engage in data analytics to form perspectives based on the external environment and situations we confront. When multiple individuals within a society adopt similar perspectives or when a collective perspective emerges from amalgamating various viewpoints, it reflects the prevailing outlook of that society or environment. The uniformity in behaviour among individuals within the same society signifies that human behaviour is a by-product of the perspectives prevalent in our surroundings. Often, we embrace others' perspectives without scrutinising their long-term implications, particularly if they offer immediate benefits. Consequently, we become adherents of these perspectives, commodities for the marketing strategies employed by others.

- Leader behaviour perspective: Unlike the follower behaviour perspective, the leader behaviour perspective is not an innate trait. It is constructed based on specific data points, references, or logical reasoning. For leaders, decision-making involves multiple parameters such as needs, availability, and the present situation. These decisions may at times get made without a comprehensive grasp of the long-term perspective. Many trailblazing leaders in social, corporate, and geographical spheres have harboured concealed perspectives that have wielded significant influence over our society, the environment, and human lives. Scrutinising the positive or negative impacts of such perspectives requires detailed case studies.

It's important to acknowledge that perspectives can vary widely and are influenced by various factors, such as individual experiences, cultural backgrounds, and personal beliefs. The leader behaviour perspective, which constitutes ~10% of the total, exerts a substantial influence on the follower behaviour perspective, accounting for the remaining ~90%. Perspective plays a crucial role in shaping our goals, actions, and contributions to society and the environment. While targets are explicitly defined and announced, perspectives remain veiled and contingent on our environment, behaviour, and situation. In the professional realm, openly withholding information is generally considered improper, but perspectives are inherently discreet.

I want to emphasise that there is no absolute right or wrong when it comes to different perspectives. However, striving for positive outcomes that benefit everyone often leads to pleasant surprises and appreciation. It is crucial to be cognisant and to evaluate the potential positive outcomes. Perspective should not be viewed as a negative concept; it may merely represent someone else's point of view. To truly grasp others' perspectives, we must put ourselves in their shoes and make a sincere effort to comprehend their viewpoint. In addition to knowledge, awareness, and targets, I would like to outline a few additional qualities that are required to consider perspectives:

- Open-mindedness: Approach different perspectives with an open mind, allowing for new insights and understanding.

- Empathy: Cultivate empathy and endeavour to comprehend the underlying motivations and experiences that shape different perspectives.

- Active listening: Practise active listening by paying close attention to others' perspectives without interrupting or dismissing them.

- Respectful dialogue: Engage in respectful dialogue to exchange perspectives, fostering constructive discussion and mutual learning.

- Critical thinking: Apply critical thinking skills to access different perspectives, considering their implications and potential consequences.

By incorporating these steps into our approach to perspectives, we can foster a more inclusive and comprehensive understanding of the world around us. Here are the key steps for considering and developing perspectives, along with the evaluation and deployment process:

- Define and understand the perspectives: Begin by clearly defining and understanding what perspectives are and how they influence our perception of the world.

- Identify needs: Recognise the underlying needs that drive the development of a particular perspective. Consider the societal or environmental issues the perspective aims to address.

- Assess availability: Evaluate the availability of resources, information, and support required to develop and implement the perspective effectively.

- Consider the situation: Recognise that the situation is a blend of the surrounding environment and the society in which the perspective will be implemented. Take into account the current state of affairs and the factors that may influence the perspective's success.

- Understand others' perspectives: Gain a deeper insight into the perspectives held by those around you. Practise active listening, empathise and engage in meaningful dialogue to comprehend different viewpoints.

- Reflect on your own perspective: Consider your own perspective towards society and the environment. Evaluate your beliefs, values, and goals, and consider how they align with the broader context.

- Align the first level of your perspective: Begin by aligning the initial level of our perspective with your understanding of needs and availability and the situation at hand.

- Create an architecture and blueprint: Develop a comprehensive plan and blueprint for your perspective, outlining the necessary steps, resources, and strategies needed to bring it to fruition.

- Simulate and conduct a Proof of Concept (POC): Test and simulate the perspective in a controlled environment. Conduct a POC to assess its feasibility, effectiveness, and potential impact.

- Re-align the perspective post-POC: Based on the results and feedback from the POC, refine and align the perspective to ensure it is optimised for implementation.

- Collect data and evaluate impact: Gather pertinent data and assess the perspective's influence on humanity, the environment, and society. Analyse the outcomes and make adjustments if necessary.

- Develop, innovate, and deploy: Refine the perspective further, introduce innovations as needed, and initially implement it within a close-knit group for a deeper understanding of its impact. Assess its effects on humanity, the environment, and society.

- Seek feedback: Extend the deployment to a larger group of family and friends to gather unfiltered feedback and insights. This feedback will be invaluable in refining and enhancing the perspective.

- Step-wise deployment: Gradually introduce the perspective to a larger control group or one region, evaluating its impact at each stage before going live on a broader scale.

By adhering to these steps, you can ensure a thoughtful and iterative process for developing, evaluating, and deploying products and services, all while considering their impact on humanity, the environment, and society. Indeed, the steps outlined can be applied to the development of any product or service before its commercial announcement in the market. Include perspective as an integral part of the marketing strategy to access consumer behaviour and anticipate the potential impact of the product or service launch.

By factoring in perspectives in marketing endeavours, companies can gain insights into consumer preferences, needs, and expectations. This comprehension aids in tailoring the product or service to meet customer demands and effectively conveying its value proposition. Evaluating consumer behaviour empowers organisations to make well-informed decisions regarding product positioning, messaging, and promotional activities.

Perspectives wield substantial influence in shaping consumer perceptions and influencing purchasing decisions. By integrating perspective into marketing strategies, companies can better address the diverse viewpoints held by their target audience, align their offerings with consumer values, and forge meaningful connections with customers. This approach not only heightens the likelihood of a successful product or service launch but also fosters positive relationships with consumers and enhances brand reputation.

Raw feedback refers to gathering inputs without directly impacting the surrounding environment or altering the provided data. It involves gathering feedback in its original, unaltered form, preserving its integrity and authenticity. Doing so enables an accurate analysis of the genuine impact or effectiveness of a product, service, or perspective, free from bias or external influence.

Obtaining raw feedback is crucial, as it offers a view of the stakeholders' opinions and experiences. It ensures that the feedback remains uninfluenced by external factors or preconceived notions. This type of feedback allows for a more precise evaluation of real-world impact and aids in pinpointing areas for improvement or further development.

To gather raw feedback, it is essential to create an environment where stakeholders feel at ease expressing their honest opinions without fear of judgment or consequences. Anonymous feedback systems or confidential channels can be implemented to encourage open and candid responses. The feedback received can then be analysed and utilised to make well-informed decisions, refine strategies, and enhance the overall quality and impact of the product, service, or perspective. By collecting raw feedback, organisations can gain invaluable insights, identify potential issues or opportunities, and continually enhance their offerings while minimising any unintended impacts on the environment or data integrity.

Understanding perspectives provides us with logical reasoning, allowing us to introspect before propagating any biased thought processes based on our unique situations, environments, and societal viewpoints. In today's era of social media, biased thought processes can be detrimental, particularly when disseminated to socially disconnected individuals. Many individuals tend to pass judgment based on biased or unbiased views they encounter on social media. Consequently, biased thoughts, products, and services can have significant impact on our society and its future in various respects.

Society furnishes us with the environment in which we develop, and that environment contributes to our awareness and knowledge. Esteemed institutions like the IITs, IIMs and MIT have flourished due to the conducive environment and awareness they foster. Likewise, most of the big organisations have become successful organisations in India or the world due to the environments in which they operate.

While we may not be able to alter others' perspectives, we can educate ourselves about those viewpoints and align our own perspectives with them and those of our society. We may not have the power to transform society as a whole, but we can raise awareness about the right perspectives.

For example, consider how Surf became a renowned detergent brand and Dish TV gained recognition for its DTH services. We have the opportunity to establish our positive perspective as a brand dedicated to humanity, the environment, and society. **As educated citizens, it is our responsibility to adopt a 360-degree positive perspective for society, showcasing our personal brand to the world, and contributing to the betterment of others. It's important to note that this contribution should extend beyond social media platforms. Engaging in meaningful actions and interactions offline can have a more profound and lasting impact on society.**

While it is true that many social issues in India have been addressed and resolved by leaders in the post-independence era, some political parties still focus on solving these out dated problems, which are no longer relevant to society. This misalignment between the issues being addressed and the current needs of society impedes progress. One can observe the changes that have unfolded in cities over the past century. Factories and cloth mills, once prominent, have become obsolete in the face of the growing demand for infrastructure and high-end residences. This illustrates how perspectives evolve, presenting new opportunities in different domains.

Agriculture is another sector in which perspective has not kept pace in India with the changing times. While it remains essential for food production, the lack of automation and rising costs have led to a decline in the quality of produce year after year. The perspective on farming remains fragmented among farmers, regional and local state governments, and the central government. Without a unified perspective and necessary changes, we may face shortages in quality food despite economic growth. It is crucial to prioritise the need for high-quality food alongside the development of infrastructure, 5G technology, FTTx, high-speed trains, and smart cities, taking into consideration the broader social perspective.

Aligning perspectives with the present time and identifying the most pressing issues allows for more effective and relevant solutions to be implemented. Adapting perspectives and embracing change enables societies to address emerging challenges and seize new opportunities for progress.

However, fast-moving perspectives can sometimes hinder innovation, leading to shortcuts or imitations. In current era innovation may prioritize expedience, copying/reverse engineering or overlooking potentially harmful effects on human lives. Examples include opting for brick houses instead of mud houses, using multiple colours instead of just white, surrounding ourselves with multiple wireless signals within our homes, and employing heavy fertiliser use to increase grain production. Individually, these choices may seem inconsequential, but their cumulative impact can become significant and detrimental.

To address this, it is crucial to pause and reflect on our approach towards innovation. We can draw valuable lessons from older civilisations and embrace a more natural lifestyle with gradual growth. It is essential to analyse the purity of the food products we use and adopt sustainable practices step by step. Instead of solely focusing on centralised development, we should aim for decentralisation of growth and development till village level.

Few case Study and Example of Perspective:

This involves creating model villages that prioritise natural elements over modernisation and shifting some basic resources to rural areas to enhance resource distribution and improve the sustainability of human lives. This approach would create a balanced relationship between metros, cities, smart cities, and villages. Additionally, it is important to provide options that cater to both modern and healthy lifestyles, allowing individuals to make choices that promote their well-being. By taking a more holistic approach and considering the long-term impacts on health and sustainability, we can work towards creating a society that balances progress and innovation with the preservation of natural elements and the well-being of individuals.

Each human body possesses unique DNA and an incredible amount of energy. The key lies in harnessing this energy and directing it towards the right goals with the right perspective. It is indeed possible to achieve remarkable outcomes by living in a village, residing in a mud house, and creating an environment of pure air and water and good-quality food.

Allow me to emphasise a hard truth: if you are not involved in creating or controlling your own food chain, and if you are not conscious of it in your daily life and work, you are the subject or product of the influences and perspectives of others. It is important to validate information and not overlook smaller data points that can validate larger impacts. In today's world, everything comes at a cost, and it is crucial to recognise that everyone is making gains or profits at the expense of someone or something else.

By acknowledging and actively participating in our own food chain and daily lives, we gain a greater sense of control over our well-being and reduce our dependence on external forces. This perspective prompts us to consider the environmental, ethical, and health-related aspects of our food choices and take responsibility for them.

Understanding the interconnectedness of our choices and the impact they have on us, others, and the world around us is a vital aspect of shaping a positive perspective. By valuing smaller data points and considering the broader implications, we can make informed decisions that align with our values and contribute to a more sustainable and equitable future.

2. WAR OF PERSPECTIVES

Every society, organisation, and individual aspires to grow. Everyone sets targets and strives to achieve them for their own growth. In today's rapidly evolving world, we are constantly moving towards adopting the perspectives of individuals, organisations, or businesses. However, we need to move away from a mindset that allows growth, money, and self-development to overshadow everything else. In contemporary times, the words 'target', 'growth' and 'achievement' hold immense power, not just within organisations but also within the lives of individuals. Each person now sets their own targets for growth and development, creating perspectives accordingly. Unfortunately, this has resulted in a trap known as "The war of perspectives", which can be equated to intense competition. This war of perspectives is evident at various levels—between countries, corporations, states, cities, families, individuals, political parties, governments, and institutions. Understanding the complexity of these competing perspectives and the intricate interactions between them becomes crucial to achieving successful outcomes. Only by comprehending and acknowledging the intricate interactions between these perspectives can we truly achieve winning results. It is essential to strike a balance between growth and considerations related to the environment, society, and individual well-being.

Let's use an example from cricket to illustrate the importance of understanding a batsman's perspective vis-a-vis a bowler. To score more runs, the batsman must consider numerous attributes and factors:

- Place: The location and conditions of the cricket ground can affect the game.

- Environment: External factors like crowd noise and atmosphere can impact the batsman's concentration.

- Pitch: The condition of the pitch—whether it's favourable to batting or aiding the bowler—plays a crucial role.

- Bowler's situation: Understanding the form and the recent performances of the bowler helps the batsman anticipate their strategy.

- Weather: Weather conditions, such as wind and humidity, can influence the ball's movement and bounce.

- Video analysis: Studying the bowler's previous matches through videos can provide insights into their bowling techniques.

- Personal problems: Knowing whetherthe bowler is dealing with any personal issues might offer clues about their mindset during the match.

- Tactical considerations: Considering the match situation and the team's overall performance helps in making tactical decisions.

- Eating habits: The batsman's diet and energy levels can affect their performance on the field.

Many more....

These attributes, among many others, need to be analysed theoretically to understand the bowler's pace, style, and perspective accurately. Experienced and skilled batsmen can quickly assess these factors in a fraction of a second, allowing them to respond appropriately and play as expected. No machine can match the natural human skill involved in delivering results in real time. Machines always need to learn before delivering results whereas human intelligence always delivers fresh results. The example also applies to understanding the perspective needed to compete effectively in the market. To achieve better results, two approaches exist: either to meticulously analyse thousands of attributes or perspectives related to the problem or to possess natural skills and instincts to resolve the problem instinctively. Both methods have their merits and can lead to successful outcomes.

The relationship between the social environment, society's needs, and corporate business is intricate and plays a crucial role in shaping our communities and economies. Let's explore this relationship:

- Social environment: The social environment encompasses the interactions, relationships, and norms that define the society in which we live. It includes cultural values, beliefs, and practices, as well as the overall well-being and quality of life of the people.

♦ Society's needs: Society has various needs, including basic necessities like food, water, shelter, healthcare, education, and safety. Additionally, it requires infrastructure, employment opportunities, environmental sustainability, and access to essential services.

♦ Corporate business: Corporations are instrumental in driving economic activities and producing goods and services to meet consumer demands. They play a significant role in generating employment, contributing to the economy, and fulfilling various societal needs through their products and services.

The dynamics of this relationship can have both positive and negative impacts on society. Individual perspective, behaviour, and actions serve as the fundamental reflections of both individual and societal perspectives in decision-making, environmental considerations, meeting consumer needs, and conducting business.

As we become more aware and competitive, we tend to create our own environments and focus solely on our individual perspectives. However, it is crucial to remember and adhere to the basic principles that govern society. While finalising the perspective and fixing the target, we should consider the well-being of not only ourselves but also the entire planet, Mother Earth, our continent, country, state, city, village, and the lives of people around us.

In the pursuit of target-driven markets, we must take the time to understand genuine needs and perspectives around us. For instance, we often pay for resources like soil, water, and air, even though they are naturally available for free on our planet. Our actions, such as polluting natural water sources, lead to the need for purified water and air purifiers in our homes, turning these necessities into commodities. Although we have the option to relocate to places with purer and more freely available resources, we often choose to stay in crowded areas for the sake of convenience. It appears that many individuals fall into the trap of not seeing, not listening, and not speaking their minds, and instead blindly following the trends of ease and convenience in their day-to-day activities. This can include seeking social status and constantly posting photos on social media platforms. There might be various reasons for falling into this trap, but one thing is certain: as we become more engrossed in these activities, we end up feeling more disconnected from society.

The essence of society lies in its connections and the understanding that not everything will be suitable for everyone. It is crucial to reflect on how often we physically connect with others or engage in face-to-face interactions rather than relying solely on social media. We might observe that the definition of being a part of society is evolving due to the increasing prominence of social media connections. We may realise that this shift is gradually redefining the concept of civics, as humans are transitioning from social animals to social media animals.

Connecting with people physically demands time and effort, while social media offers a quick and convenient means of communication through various modes like unicast, multicast, or broadcast. These fundamental changes in human behaviour are significantly impacting our society, humanity, and the environment at a rapid pace.

To maintain a balanced society, it is vital to recognise the value of genuine human connections. While technology and social media have their merits, we must not let them overshadow the importance of meaningful face-to-face interactions and genuine human relationships. By embracing both aspects of communication, we can ensure a more harmonious and well-connected society, benefiting both individuals and the broader community.

These changes in behaviour and perspectives have significant implications for our society, humanity, and the environment. We must strive to strike a balance between technological advancements and maintaining genuine human connections. By doing so, we can ensure sustainable and harmonious coexistence for all.

Once again, electronic media has become a massive advertisement platform, leading to social disconnection due to our own imaginary perceptions of either our current status or the desire to become someone else. Consider the impact of continually posting good morning messages to all our connections on social media. Each individual message may seem insignificant, but when multiplied by millions of people, the messages turn into a significant amount of data stored in data centres. This data storage requires physical resources, such as energy and equipment, which have a limited lifespan and eventually contribute to energy waste.

The marketing trap lies in the fact that we become socially disconnected while being engrossed in trying to achieve our own perceptions by posting pictures, thoughts, and posts without truly engaging with others. This scenario is common worldwide, and while it may be acceptable at times, it is not necessarily the best approach most of the time.

When we share something on social media, it becomes accessible to all, including unknown individuals. As a result, we inadvertently advertise products and services without fully understanding their impact on others. This can lead to mixed reactions from the audience—some may appreciate it while others may feel negatively about it. It becomes a virtual trap for all social media users.

To counter this trend, it is essential to offer products and services that align with the needs of our environment, society, family, and friends. When developing anything, we must not forget the basic principle of connecting people socially. The focus should be on fostering real connections rather than promoting disconnection through virtual interactions. I encourage physical connections over relying solely on virtual ones through social media apps or video calls. While these apps may connect us, they are developed based onthe developer's logic, and we end up using tools that skew towards the app developers' perspectives rather than our own. By following the basics and developing our own logic, we can make genuine connections and engage directly with others.

In conclusion, let's be mindful of the impact of electronic media on our social connections and prioritise meaningful interactions that foster genuine connections with the people around us. To counteract these effects and maintain genuine social connections, it is essential for an individual to be mindful of the influence of electronic media and its potential impact on their perceptions and behaviour. Here are some suggestions:

- ♦ Be authentic: Instead of trying to conform to societal expectations or projecting an idealised version of yourself, focus on being authentic and true to your values and interests.

- ♦ Limit media exposure: Set boundaries for media consumption, especially on social media platforms. Recognise that the content is often curated and may not represent reality accurately.

- ♦ Prioritiseface-to-face interaction: Make an effort to engage in meaningful face-to-face interactions with family, friends, and the community. These interactions foster genuine connections and emotional well-being.

♦ Practise gratitude: Cultivate a sense of gratitude for what you have instead of constantly striving for more. Appreciating the present moment and simple pleasures can lead to greater contentment.

♦ Seek balance: Balance virtual interactions with real-life experiences. Spend time outdoors, pursue hobbies, and engage in activities that bring you joy and fulfilment.

♦ Filter media content: Be critical of the advertisements and content you consume. Filter out unrealistic portrayals and focus on content that inspires, educates, and uplifts.

♦ Engage in purposeful use: Use electronic media purposefully for learning, staying informed, and connecting with others positively.

By being mindful of the influence of electronic media and making conscious choices about its impact on our lives, we can maintain genuine social connections, foster a healthier sense of self, and strive for a more balanced and fulfilling existence.

As a technical person at my core, I follow a universal truth from instrumentation: error always exists, and it cannot be entirely eliminated, but it can be minimised. This truth extends to various aspects of human life as well. In the context of a developing nation, the concepts of right and wrong are subjective and dependent on individual perspectives or derived behaviour. Thus, it is essential not to blame others for our own perceptions of what is right or wrong. Instead, we should acknowledge the inherent subjectivity and diverse viewpoints that shape our beliefs and actions. Understanding this truth allows us to approach situations with more empathy, open-mindedness, and willingness to learn from one another's perspectives.

According to psychology, 75% of an individual's behaviour is influenced by environmental factors and 25% by genetic factors. Coming from a consumer behaviour background, I can confidently assert that, in society today, more than 75% of people base their behaviours on the perspectives of others and are heavily influenced by targets and goals of others through various media. The remaining people may be uncertain about their role. Upon observing the steps involved in our actions, we often realise that our behaviours and subsequent actions are influenced by specific targeting aimed at eliciting certain responses from us. While there's nothing inherently wrong with being targeted, the issue is that we often overlook our core values and the impact of our actions on natural resources, the environment, and the society. It is crucial to be precise and considerate when making decisions, rather than simply going with the flow or following the crowd. We tend to make basic mistakes until we reach a threshold at which corrective action becomes difficult or even impossible. In the game of perspectives, awareness and the number of followers you have play a significant role. The more people who follow you, the more powerful you may become, which can in itself become a trap.

Life follows a natural progression, encompassing various aspects such as knowledge, education, and experience. I consider myself fortunate to have witnessed the transformation of India into a developing country in the post-1991 era. I have been exposed to multiple developing environments, including hardware, software, media, consumer products, the digital, big data and consumer behaviour worlds, as well as industries like cable TV, DTH, and broadcast. Being part of a developing nation has allowed us to experience significant changes and advancements, In contrast, developed countries often focus their resources on specialised areas with high precision and accuracy. The developed country scope of exploration may be limited unless they actively seek out new challenges and go beyond established norms. For developed country what we experienced in 1991 may be akin to events from 1891 or even earlier. Developed countries may find themselves immune to the layers of targeting that developing nations encounter, leading potentially to complacency in their approach.

To break free from this stagnation, developed countries must be willing to explore different avenues and think outside the box. They may need to invest more efforts in pursuing new skills and ventures beyond their established products or services. This openness to innovation and willingness to go the extra mile can help them avoid becoming confined to a limited set of options.

In conclusion, every nation's journey is unique, and changes to lifestyles vary across different environments. While developing countries may have faced rapid changes and development, developed countries can learn from their experiences and actively seek out new challenges to continue their growth and evolution. By embracing innovation and breaking free from the constraints of traditional practices, developed countries can shape their own paths and stay relevant in an ever-changing world.

Having been involved in human behaviour measurement and studied various books, I have come to the conclusion that many trade wars are driven by the powerful pursuit of specific goals or objectives. This war of perspective applies to individuals, companies, categories, brands, institutes, countries, and various entities. The existence of loopholes and the lack of effective checks and balances contribute to the escalation of these conflicts. The results of such accumulation become evident in major crises like global warming, water scarcity, and the degradation of the Earth, which is turned it into a dumping ground for waste. Current compliance standards often focus on specific parameters without thoroughly analysing their broader impact. Small changes that go unnoticed or unaddressed can accumulate over time, leading to crises. Certifications and regulations may not adequately address the long-term consequences on our natural resources and the preservation for future and human life.

To address these challenges, a more comprehensive and far-sighted approach is required. We need to consider the full lifecycle of our actions and decisions, taking into account their potential consequences on the environment and society. By prioritising sustainable practices and investing in long-term strategies, we can work towards avoiding catastrophic outcomes and safeguarding the well-being of future generations. It is essential to create and enforce regulations that genuinely protect our natural resources and encourage responsible behaviours across all levels of society, from individuals to large corporations and governments.

Unnoticed impact of war of perspective:

Let's consider the example of a mobile brand that sells handsets and services. The average life of a mobile device is around two years, and the total number of mobile devices consumed on our planet is approximately 15 billion, including dual device usage. The disposal of 15 billion mobile devices every two years poses a significant environmental hazard. Despite widespread awareness about this issue, no concrete actions have been taken to address it. This pattern extends to other electronic devices like TVs, refrigerators, air conditioners, laptops, automobiles, and more. The lack of proper recycling and responsible post-use practices is evident.

Companies have sophisticated softwares for managing the product lifecycle while the device is functional, but there is a lack of softwares or systems to track these devices and materials after they are disposed of, recycled, or decomposed. Consequently, waste ends up being dumped indiscriminately without any effective tracking system in place. This problem is particularly pronounced in developed countries.

To address this issue, it is essential to introduce a comprehensive and uniform approach applicable to all users. Devices should be designed to last for at least two generations, and recycling should be encouraged in different forms, with individuals taking responsibility for the proper disposal of their devices. A robust tracking system should be established to monitor these devices from purchase to end-of-life or decommissioning, ensuring full user responsibility.

Solution examples of existing problems:

Implementing a mandatory exchange system, whereby users can only purchase new devices after submitting their old ones for proper recycling, could significantly reduce careless dumping. Additionally, setting clear parameters for material recycling will further discourage irresponsible disposal practices.

Taking such measures will not only benefit the environment but also make new electronic goods more cost-effective in the long run, as the cost of proper disposal is factored into the purchase price. It is crucial to take action collectively to address this pressing environmental issue and create a sustainable approach to electronic device usage and disposal.

We have raised a crucial point about the need for certifying devices to ensure safe usage and recyclability. Indeed, a lack of foresight and consideration for the end-of-life impact of products has led to an alarming increase in dumping grounds near cities, as well as the dumping of waste into the seas. This accumulation of waste is placing severe strains on our environment and making many cities and areas unsafe to live in.

To address this issue, it is imperative to adopt a more comprehensive and responsible perspective vis-a-vis product development and usage. Certification processes should be designed not only to ensure safe usage but also to evaluate the recyclability and environmental impact of devices throughout their lifecycle.

Learning from the successes and failures of developed countries can provide valuable insights and lessons on how to effectively manage waste and create sustainable practices. Both success and failure stories have valuable lessons to offer, highlighting the importance of making informed decisions and adopting a proactive approach to environmental conservation.

While advancements in technology and the exploration of other planets are essential for human progress, we must not overlook the pressing issues we face on our own planet. Instead of searching for life on other planets, we must prioritise the preservation of life on Earth and work collectively to create a safer and more sustainable environment for current and future generations.

By rethinking our perspectives, acknowledging the hidden costs of unsustainable practices, and implementing responsible measures, we can mitigate the damage to our environment and create a more harmonious relationship with the planet we call home. It is crucial for individuals, corporations, and governments to come together, take accountability, and take steps towards building a better future for our society, environment, and world.

The perspective discussed earlier, which prioritises adopting innovations that were introduced by earlier generations and being cautious about blindly following the latest technological trends, is indeed valid. Instead of merely copying or imitating what others have done, it is essential to have a more thoughtful and mindful approach to innovation. Starting the innovation process at the beginning, considering our unique conditions as human beings, society, and the environment, is crucial. By understanding the natural processes and the actual needs of our surroundings, we can develop innovations that are more relevant, sustainable, and beneficial to our society and the planet. Innovation should not be driven by the desire to be up-to-date or to replicate what has been done elsewhere. Rather, it should involve a thorough analysis of the potential benefits and draw backs of any new technology or idea. Understanding the pros and cons, and how they align with our values and priorities, can help us make more informed decisions about which innovations to embrace and which to avoid. By taking a conscious and responsible approach to innovation, we can avoid blindly becoming followers and, instead, become active contributors to positive change. Embracing our unique perspectives, considering our own conditions, and innovating with a focus on sustainability and social impact can lead to solutions that are truly transformative and make a difference in the world.

Let us move forward with open minds, critical thinking, and a commitment to building a better future for ourselves and the generations to come. Millions of perspectives will exist in our surroundings; we need to learn to emerge from the 'War of perspectives' with flying colours.

3. THE CONSUMER BEHAVIOUR PERSPECTIVE

From a consumer behaviour perspective, the primary goal is to gain maximum value from the products and services offered by institutions or organisations. To achieve this, it is crucial to understand the actual needs of customers and their behaviour in the market place to support our customers as expected.

Consumer behaviour refers to the study of how individuals make decisions regarding the purchase, use, and disposal of goods, services, and ideas. It involves analysing factors that influence consumer choices, such as personal preferences, motivations, perceptions, attitudes, cultural influences, advertisements, and social interactions. By understanding consumer behaviour, organisations can tailor their offerings to align with the needs and desires of their target customers. This knowledge allows companies to develop products and services that meet customer expectations, provide relevant features and benefits, and deliver a positive customer experience.

Consumer behaviour research can be based on a number of methodologies, including surveys, interviews, focus groups, observation, and data analysis. These help organisations identify patterns and trends and gain insights into consumer preferences and purchasing decisions. By gaining a deep understanding of consumer behaviour, organisations can design effective marketing strategies, develop compelling brand messaging, optimise pricing strategies, improve product design, enhance customer service, and create targeted advertising campaigns. This knowledge helps companies maximise their turnover, revenue, and profit margins by delivering products and services that resonate with their customers.

The complete ecosystem of businesses, organisations, and industries revolves around meeting current needs and maximising gains. In a market-driven economy, businesses strive to identify and fulfil the demands and desires of consumers to generate profits and grow. It is true that organisations have a significant impact on society as they serve large numbers of people through their products, services, and operations. Individual consumers typically have limited influence over the broader social impact of a product or service. Organisations have the resources, scale, and ability to analyse and assess the impact of their actions from long-term and social perspectives.

The collection and analysis of data have become widespread across various industries and sectors, including business, politics, and healthcare. Companies now recognise the value of data and employ various methods to gather it, aiming to understand consumer behaviour and target customers based on their actual needs.

In the business world, data collection helps companies personalise their marketing efforts and improve customer experiences. By analysing customer data, businesses can gain insights into consumer preferences, purchasing patterns, and behaviours, allowing them to tailor their products and services accordingly. This can lead to more effective targeting and increased customer satisfaction.

Similarly, political parties utilise data to target specific voter segments. By analysing data on voter demographics, interests, and preferences, political campaigns can customise their messages and strategies to appeal to different voter groups. This approach aims to maximise the effectiveness of their campaigns and influence voter behaviour vis-a-vispolitical parties.

In the healthcare sector, data analysis plays a crucial role in providing personalised care and improving health outcomes. By analysing patient data, health systems can identify patterns, trends, and risk factors, enabling them to deliver targeted interventions and treatments. This data-driven approach aims to enhance patient care and optimise healthcare delivery.

The data that companies collect from primary sources, including viewership data, traffic data, individual movement data, purchase data, and various forms of detection data like facial, object, and logo recognition, provide valuable insights to businesses and organisations. Additionally, there are secondary sources of derived data that enable actions, predictions, patterns, graphs, and plans. Through data analysis and interpretation, organisations can extract meaningful information and make informed decisions to optimise their operations and offerings. Traditional factors like region, culture, language, age, and gender, which were previously used to define consumer behaviour, have taken a backseat compared to the data generated from actions such as what individuals do, view, and say and where they go. This suggests that actual behaviours and actions have become more influential in understanding consumer behaviour than demographic or socio-cultural factors.

However, it is important to recognise that the collection and utilisation of personal data raises concerns about privacy, surveillance, and the ethical implications of data usage. While data-driven approaches can bring benefits, there is a need to balance them with the protection of individual privacy rights and the responsible handling of personal information. Responsible data collection and usage should adhere to legal frameworks, respect privacy rights, and ensure the security and confidentiality of individuals' personal information, and individuals must be mindful of their actions and surveillance by powerful entities, systems, and technologies. It is also important for organisations and institutions to prioritise understanding the actual problems and needs of individuals and communities, rather than solely focusing on their own targets or agendas. Balancing personal growth and technological advancements on the one hand and, on the other, maintaining our humanity, social connections, and environmental well-being, being aware of the implications of our actions and advocating responsible data practices, can contribute to a more ethical and sustainable use of data in society.

The development of centralised air conditioning systems and unified technological solutions for homes, offices, and travel further highlights the integration of technology into our environments. These advancements aim to enhance convenience, efficiency, and comfort, streamlining our experiences across different spaces. While technology brings numerous benefits, it's important to be aware of the potential implications and challenges that arise from our increasing dependence on it. This includes concerns related to privacy, security, data protection, and the potential impact on social interactions and personal well-being. Maintaining a balanced approach and being mindful of our reliance on technology can help us navigate its influence effectively. It's crucial to consider our individual needs, preferences, and the potential consequences of our technological choices to ensure that technology, rather than being something that dominates our lives, serves as a tool to enhance our lives. As technology continues to evolve, it's important for individuals, organisations, and society as a whole to critically evaluate its impact, promote responsible use, and foster a healthy relationship between humans and technology. Top of Form Technology is driven by business and businesses need information. No policy binds technology to collect data with your consent. **We make policies for governance, innovation, Information Technology—we make it and technology can break it for business.**

Impacts:

As mentioned earlier, the storage and processing of data, whether in physical data centres or cloud-based infrastructure, require significant resources, such as electricity, processing power, and cooling systems. The operation of data centres, which house the infrastructure that enables the storage, management, and analysis of vast amounts of data, consumes a significant amount of electricity and can generate heat. To maintain optimal conditions for the equipment and prevent overheating, data centres often rely on air conditioning or cooling systems. This can result in substantial energy consumption and contribute to the generation of waste heat. Social media platforms have become popular avenues for sharing photos and gaining likes and comments. However, it is important to consider the broader implications of these activities and the environmental costs associated with them.

Practices that can minimise the negative environmental impact of digital activities include:

- ♦ Conscious consumption: Reflecting on the necessity and purpose of sharing photos and considering alternative ways to connect and communicate.

- ♦ Optimising file sizes: Compressing images and using efficient file formats to reduce data size and bandwidth requirements.

- ♦ Responsible data storage: Using cloud storage services that prioritise energy efficiency and sustainability practices.

- ♦ Internet infrastructure: Supporting and advocating the development of eco-friendly telecommunication networks and data centres that prioritise renewable energy sources.

- ♦ Recycling and proper disposal: Ensuring the responsible recycling or disposal of electronic devices to reduce electronic waste.

- ◆ Awareness and education: Promoting awareness about the environmental impact of digital activities and encouraging sustainable practices among individuals and communities.

It's important to note that addressing these concerns requires collective efforts from individuals, organisations, and policymakers. From an individual perspective, it's important to be aware of the potential risks and implications of sharing personal data and to make informed choices about the platforms and services we engage with. Being mindful of our digital footprint and advocating privacy rights and responsible data practices can contribute to a more balanced and sustainable approach to data-driven targeting.

Ultimately, it is crucial for both organisations and individuals to consider the broader ethical, environmental, and social impacts of data collection and utilisation. By promoting responsible data practices, we can strive for a more sustainable and respectful use of technology and personal information. Top of Form

Uses:

The usage of data from different sources shapes perspective. Data about human actions, like household or individual content viewing behaviour, are tracked through DTH, cable TV, OTT applications, or any devices, applications, and services we use. **What we watch, when we watch, on what device we watch, where we watch, and who we are—everything is tracked to establish behaviour patterns and create blocks of similar behaviour and promote similar products and services.** Service providers track our viewing time, the type, genre, and language of the content we view, and our location, after which millions of attributes are generated out of the data and we are targeted with ads for FMCG, kitchenware, cosmetics, electronic gadgets, automobiles, etc. I have a single question: is tracking all these behaviours and selling commodities for two years worth putting so great an indirect load on Mother Earth in terms of the whole IT infra net? The process of selling things is so complex that quality and compliance become formalities. **We should be inventing easy buying and selling methods and introducing natural processes in between. Correction is needed at every stage, from product development and innovation to selling and buying techniques.**

Effect:

In effect, we are following the theory of the disconnected world, where by everyone is disconnected from each other and targeted in silos through the application of multiple marketing methods. Instead, we can easily follow the old Indian mantra of distributed markets and connected people. In the olden days, there were smaller market regions and the actual needs of people were understood through everyday engagement.

We need to understand that human behaviour is driven by 'ease of doing things'. The same principle applies here to the ease of selling products and services using technology and consumer data collected at the back end. The above example shows how customer behaviour is driven by technology, and it fails the basic principle that the customer (not technology) is God.

Technology can disconnect us from direct personal interactions and our own inner voice. We often turn to technology for guidance, analysis, and validation, instead of relying on our own thoughts, intuition, and direct human connections. This heavy reliance on external sources, such as deep conviction advertisements or data analysis, can shape our decision-making processes and actions. We may overlook our own internal cues and perspectives, which can lead to a disconnection from our true needs, values, and desires.

The consumer behaviour perspective arises when we are socially disconnected and fully dependent on technology to understand others' behaviours. That we analyse our own behaviour through technology indicates the extent of our dependency. We stop thinking about our inner voice and directly interacting with others to make decisions. We analyse our external environment, which is replaced with others' perspectives, through deep conviction advertisements and decide our course of action. **Honesty and trust become commodities, and you have to pay for them. Marrying and having kids become optional. These are the hard truths of our current society—we are forgetting the basics of social science.** In this kind of world, you need to be prepared to make the right decision, thinking about short-term and long-term impacts. Don't take decisions for the short term and damage human life. While we must adopt new advanced technologies, we must do so while keeping the basic principle of social connection intact.

There are indeed alternative approaches to buying and selling that are more sustainable and in line with natural processes. Re-evaluating product development and innovation, as well as the marketing and distribution techniques used, can help align them with more environmentally-friendly practices. Additionally, considering traditional market methodologies, such as engaging with customers on a personal level and understanding their actual needs through interactions, can be valuable in creating a more connected and customer-centric approach. Ensuring the quality of marketing attributes is also essential, as maintaining accurate and relevant information is crucial to providing value to customers and reducing wasteful targeting efforts. Developing products and services based on genuine customer insights obtained through surveys, focus groups, and customer engagement can help ensure that those products and surveys align with real user requirements. Design thinking, which emphasises empathy and understanding the user's perspective, can be a valuable approach in product development. By putting the customer at the centre of the process, teams can create solutions that truly address their needs and provide value.

Sustainable design practices that can be integrated into the product development process to minimise negative environmental effects include the choice of materials, durability, recyclability, and the potential for reuse or repurposing. Encouraging the development of products that have a long life span and are designed for easy recycling or minimal environmental impact is vital.

Extending the usable life of products can reduce waste and contribute to a more sustainable environment. Furthermore, innovation teams should take a holistic approach, considering not only the immediate impact of the product but also its long-term consequences. This involves evaluating the environmental and social impacts throughout the entire lifecycle of the product, from raw material extraction to disposal. By adopting sustainable design principles, organisations can create products that are not only aligned with customer needs but also contribute to a more sustainable future. Prioritising longevity, recyclability, and minimal environmental impact can help create a more sustainable environment for all.

The perspective of consumer behaviour has shifted towards technology, fostering social disconnection and prioritising the fast achievement of targets. However, it's essential to directly engage with customers to comprehend their needs, utilise technology to support them, and ensure the long-term sustainability of our business for the benefit of society, the environment, and individuals. True comprehension and application of the consumer behaviour perspective as a core principle are essential for achieving these objectives.

4. DILUTING CUSTOMER'S PERSPECTIVE

The current business landscape is dominated by a generation with an intense focus on its perspective, making it challenging for others to compete. If this approach is ethical, it poses no issues, but reliance on marketing, communication, or public relation management alone can lead to perilous outcomes. Businesses must engage customers openly, understanding their viewpoints accurately. Diluting the customer's perspective is a risky proposition and this dilution is exacerbated by technology's role in potentially distorting these perspectives. While technology enhances personalised interactions, it also risks being misused for manipulation or privacy violations.

Direct customer engagement is essential to safeguarding customers' perspectives. It should be a top priority for businesses; otherwise, customers might refrain from providing honest feedback or voicing concerns against any wrong doing. Without genuine feedback, it becomes challenging to improve and develop future products and services according to the customers' needs. Businesses need to decide whether to prioritise short-term gains or long-term needs. A common problem in current business approaches is the tendency to start with fixed, pre-defined targets or perspectives based on virtual data. This indicates that we often begin with preconceived answers or solutions to problems without fully understanding the actual issues or requirements. In contrast, feedback should begin with a blank page, allowing us to understand the actual requirements of customers or the raw problems they face.

The customer life cycle has evolved, transitioning from direct engagement to structured approaches, visual advertisements, video clips, big data analytics, and precision targeting. While technology enhances marketing, maintaining a balance between targeted efforts and respecting customer privacy is vital. Let's delve into the key stages of this progression:

1. Raw facts and needs: In the past, businesses engaged with customers directly and drew insights from raw facts and observations to understand their needs and preferences. This was a more personalised and hands-on approach.

2. Engagement and understanding: With time, businesses started to focus on actively engaging with customers through discussions and interactions. This allowed them to gain a deeper understanding of customer needs, pain points, and feedback.

3. Surveys and specific questions: The next step involved implementing more structured approaches, such as customer surveys and targeted questions. These methods aimed to draw out specific views and opinions from customers to inform decision-making.

4. Visual advertisements: With the rise of mass media and technology, businesses started using visual elements like hoardings, banners, and advertisements to reach a broader audience and promote their products or services.

5. Video clips and targeted advertising: As technology advanced further, businesses embraced video clips and targeted advertising to capture consumers' attention and deliver more compelling messages.

6. Big data analytics: The advent of big data allowed businesses to gather and analyse vast amounts of customer data, enabling them to understand customer behaviour, preferences, and trends on a larger scale.

7. Precision targeting: Today, businesses leverage sophisticated data analytics and tracking technologies to follow consumers across various platforms and tailor their marketing messages with precision, based on consumer movements, behaviours, and interests.

This progression reflects the ongoing quest to better understand and engage customers, utilising technology and data to refine targeting strategies. While advancements in technology have allowed for more effective marketing and personalisation, it's essential to strike a balance between targeted marketing and respecting customer privacy and preferences.

As businesses continue to evolve their customer engagement strategies, ethical considerations and transparent communication will remain critical factors in building trust and maintaining long-term customer relationships. Understanding customer needs and providing value-driven solutions will always be at the core of successful businesses, irrespective of technological advancements.

However, the current trend is limiting customers' decision-making abilities by offering products through a 360-degree social network, hindering unbiased thinking. Mapping customer information with socio-demographic data using machine learning risks diluting human intelligence. While prediction models offer accuracy, reliance on technology could stall progress. Striking a balance between technology and human intelligence is essential for sustainable growth.

According to the basic principle of instrumentation, 'error always exists', but the current prediction models can work with maximum accuracy until new innovations/changes arise. In contrast, technology cannot predict without errors, whereas human intelligence can. While current prediction models may not be damaging individual perspectives or needs, society will not progress further without the natural human behaviour of innovating for change. Embracing change and adopting new experiences, even with the possibility of failure, is essential for growth. However, excessive dependence on technology could lead to a halt in the progress of humanity, society, and the environment.

My suggestion is not to stop innovating, but rather to ensure an accurate understanding of customer requirements through proper market research. It is crucial to carefully consider the impact on human life, society, and the environment when deploying technology. Applying design thinking and conducting simulations of innovations before rollouts can help with the assessment of potential consequences. By doing so, we can create a space where both artificial intelligence and human intelligence can coexist and thrive in harmony. We need to embrace technology while also allowing ample space for human intelligence to make decisions about success or failure and to explore new areas. Failing to strike this balance could lead to a deadlock in the market, product, and services.

Now a days everyone wants to make more money, but I have observed a major issue in market research. Only a few analyse the market through proper research methodologies, attempting to correct universe estimations for targeting and refining base/raw data. I am not opposed to automation, but it needs to be thoroughly tested through sampling panels, experimental panels, and design thinking. Otherwise, you are merely playing with base data, and your business will not thrive on such a foundation in the long term.

Corporate market research often prioritises business perspectives, sidelining customer voices. To ensure success, prioritising customer feedback, conducting proper market research, and optimising sales strategies are crucial. Making hasty alterations to these fundamentals can backfire. We have witnessed multiple examples of the voices of individual customers being unintentionally suppressed and success being showcased while actually facing losses. On one side, the entire system, comprising marketing communication experts, legal advisors, and consultants, aligns with the business, while, on the other side, we often find individual customers in vulnerable positions. This situation is not ideal, as businesses thrive because of customers. We should prioritise creating a better environment for our customers compared to resources hired by corporates. Although customers might raise their voices occasionally, they can't compete with the influence of the entire digital marketing and social media system.

It is the responsibility of business owners to place customers in the highest regard, adhering to the afore mentioned principle of the customer being God. While some individuals may misuse their customer status, most of the time, organisations benefit from customers' perspectives. To address cases of misuse, proper legal measures should be put in place that do not involve the use of social media. Many organisations have the means to run extensive campaigns and alter public perspectives through marketing efforts. However, what customers genuinely experience is more important than what they are forced to read or watch during marketing campaigns.

In the B2B context, data is crucial, allowing market trends to be predicted and customer behaviour to be understood. However, to derive accurate insights, we must treat data as dynamic, correcting and redefining it at every moment and mapping changes to improve accuracy continually. Direct raw data or aggregated data can become a coal mine for anyone, as it can be used according to their perspective or needs. However, when we clean and define data through pre-processing and processing rules, creating usable data becomes like a production line, with a continual focus on accuracy. This correct data becomes the foundation for further application, and its definition and essence remain unchanged. The problem arises when everyone uses the raw form of the data. On the other hand, the correct way of representing data is usable data presented in a linear form, showcasing both the coal and the diamonds together in the same location and at the same time.

Relying solely on data risks diluting customer perspectives. Usable data should be analysed, and physical connections with customers should be established to collect feedback, avoiding over reliance on automation.

Capturing customer behaviour data requires a robust process that includes metadata, method of transfer, and context. Challenges in data collection arise, impacting the quality of information. Businesses must prioritise accurate data capture and thorough processing to gain valuable insights into customer behaviour. Data acts as a communication system, and any flaw in the process can impact the quality and accuracy of information, similar to coding and decoding in technology. It is crucial to recreate data in a manner that reflects the customer's behaviour while using the services provided by the data collector. Data serves as a valuable source of information, but its accuracy is paramount. Viewing data insights as a product development process is a mistake; data is the production line, and each moment requires a fixed set of processes to generate correct and uniform usable data that can be considered as the flow of behaviour changes. This ensures that meaningful insights and products may aligned based on data insights.

However, challenges arise in the data collection process, such as errors in data collection, data continuity, capturing session-level data with correct timestamps, technical errors, fusing other relevant data sources to replicate customer behaviour, external impacts and corrections, outlier detection and correction, creating similar segments for accuracy checks, improving accuracy by creating similar universes for comparison, and showcasing all data segments to provide a comprehensive view. The trend of collecting, owning, and representing data in the modern world can sometimes divert or dilute customer perspectives due to these reasons. To overcome these challenges, organisations must prioritise accurate data capture and thorough processing to gain valuable insights into customer behaviour. To address the above challenges and preserve customer perspectives, businesses can consider the following approaches:

- ◆ Transparent communication: Clearly communicate product features, benefits, and limitations, allowing customers to make informed decisions.

- Minimal invasive marketing: Reduce intrusive advertising that overwhelms customers, and instead provide valuable content that helps customers make better choices.

- Customer education: Educate customers about the product/service features and how they align with their needs, enabling them to make well-informed decisions.

- Respect customer choice: Trust that customers can make decisions based on their individual preferences and respect their choices, even if they differ from the norm.

- Seek diverse feedback: Encourage diverse perspectives in feedback collection to ensure a comprehensive understanding of customer experiences.

- Opt-out options: Offer opt-out options for customers who prefer not to receive targeted advertisements or personalised offers.

By promoting customer autonomy, fostering transparency, and respecting their decisions, businesses can better preserve and understand genuine customer perspectives, leading to more meaningful relationships and improved customer satisfaction.

Data correction is an ongoing process that requires constant review and improvement. Customer feedback accounts for about 90% of data correction attributes. Emphasising the importance of customer feedback helps maintain a customer-centric approach and fosters innovation based on genuine customer needs and preferences.

Continuous improvement and accuracy in data correction are vital to making informed business decisions, offering enhanced services, and building lasting customer relationships. Emphasising the importance of customer feedback in the data correction process helps maintain a customer-centric approach and fosters innovation based on genuine customer needs and preferences.

5. THE INDIAN ECONOMY PERSPECTIVE

From the era of kingdoms until the 1800s, India stood as a prosperous and influential nation in the global economy, attracting business from today's so-called developed countries. Its success was attributed to the collaboration between small kingdoms, each overseeing their respective areas. However, internal conflicts among these kingdoms marked the beginning of India's decline, eventually leading to its destruction by external forces.

During this period, external influences imposed their marketing perspectives on India, aiming to dismantle its economy to favourably position their own products and services. This approach eroded the social culture, harmony, and environmental balance of the country. A sound marketing strategy involves understanding the local environment, social culture, and resources to create products that align with people's needs. Unfortunately, the impact of foreign goods and products was so severe that it crippled India's economy. Major Indian buyers and kingdoms began to prefer foreign products, leading to a decline in domestic industries. Consequently, many Indians turned to farming, and the true extent of the damage to India's economy went unnoticed by the kingdoms until it was too late.

Redundancy, cultural upheaval, and security concerns are significant factors in undermining any society. Thus, it is essential to remain vigilant, considering competition, environmental factors, social values, and product needs to deliver the right output. The practice of providing freebies as a survival tactic can be detrimental, turning individuals into commodities for others' perspectives and ultimately weakening the economy and the societal ecosystem.

Instead, the focus must be on the principle of earning to survive, based on the understanding that true growth and development cannot be achieved through handouts. By being proactive and fostering a sustainable economic environment, we can ensure long-term growth and prosperity for society as a whole.

Economic recovery faces challenges when external forces divert benefits either to foreign countries or for personal or family use. Economic growth relies on the masses, and our political system exploits them for individual or party gains rather than focusing on growing the economy for the masses.

The current political era is marked by making citizens reliant on handouts such as electricity, laptops, TVs, and pensions, distributed through direct tax collection. However, this short-sighted approach does not contribute to the long-term development of our nation. Instead of investing in building a strong and independent country, it represents a wasteful allocation of resources. Citizens, including political parties, leaders, and businesses, should be engaged in actively contributing to the economy.

A comparison between those who receive free handouts and those who earn their livelihood through work reveals that the latter are significant economic assets. Leaders should prioritise creating job opportunities as a fundamental strategy for national growth. Clear Key Performance Indicators (KPIs) should be established for the responsible utilisation of taxpayer funds, with free provisions limited to essential services such as healthcare, social assistance, or disaster relief and recovery.

Taxpayers, including those from major cities like Mumbai and Delhi, contribute substantial amounts to the government's coffers. However, instead of promoting development and elevating the masses to the next level, governments distribute free electricity, water, food, and entertainment solely to secure votes. This approach should not be mistaken for genuine development.

To clarify, I am not opposed to providing social services like education, healthcare, and food. However, these initiatives should empower individuals, and the distinction between genuine needs and societal services should be maintained, independent of government influence. Governments should not be aligned with specific political parties, and caution should be exercised in how taxpayer funds are spent. Individuals need to earn their livelihoods to ensure economic sustainability and growth. Government benefits should be directed towards those who are genuinely disabled or in need and most of the individuals should be given opportunities to work rather than just handouts.

Governments often opt for shortcuts to secure votes, using poverty alleviation and social improvement as pretexts. This trend is now observed globally, with leaders seeking to gain a loyal voter base through the distribution of basic necessities, resulting in populations becoming dependent on specific parties or governments without along-term vision. Governments should focus on fostering fair competition, encouraging citizens to transition from recipiency to contribution by creating numerous employment prospects.

In democratic countries, the constitution grants the greatest power to the public. Not everyone is a politician, so citizens must harness their power and behave as responsible members of their democratic nations. Shedding the labels of political parties will damage individuals' rights and enable them to realise their true potential and break limitations.

A significant number of Indian corporations are controlled by families, and, similarly, many local and national political parties are also led by families that come into power upon winning elections. Within our country, it is crucial to harmonise these perspectives in the process of nation-building.

Our society needs to harness the complete potential of its entire population. Due to certain overarching perspectives, not everyone in our population contributes to the growth of our economy. This presents a challenge, as every individual in India should make a meaningful contribution through their work to fortify our economy. This necessity extends across all sectors, be it personal, familial, societal, small and medium-sized enterprises (SMEs), corporations, or political parties.

Prior to liberalisation, our economic growth was heavily reliant on our own agricultural sector, which contributed the maximum of our economic expansion. After the process of liberalisation was initiated in 1991, our economy shifted its reliance onto external sources and other sectors, including advanced infrastructure, globally competitive fast-moving consumer goods (FMCGs) products, and top-tier automobile manufacturing. This transition indicates that we adopted a global marketing perspective and became ensnared in the cycle of relying on foreign products instead of cultivating our intrinsic strengths by, for instance, refining agriculture into high-quality FMCGs or advancing software development to establish our own intellectual property.

It is crucial for us to operate in parallel streams, maintaining and nurturing our existing strengths while simultaneously fostering our unique perspective. This entails safeguarding our foundational capabilities like agriculture and software development, as well as exploring untapped domains that possess the potential to capture the global market. Instead of persistently importing products, we should aspire to reach the point where the world seeks to emulate our achievements in areas like agriculture and software. It is within our reach to reverse the trend and replace external dependencies with our indigenous capabilities and offerings.

The genuine needs and aspirations of the public are a nurturing environment, robust healthcare, accessible education, a thriving society, clean air, pure water, and nutritious food. Thus, it becomes imperative for governments to prioritise the provision of health and education security to all citizens. Comprehensive infrastructure development is essential at all levels to facilitate these objectives. Government policies should be inclusive, focusing on the welfare of all individuals and communities, as any form of discrimination would only serve to fragment our society. Allowing discrimination would pave the way for certain groups to assume power and act in their own interests. This would lead to a skewed representation that wouldn't take into account the broader public's needs. The significance of health and quality food must not be overlooked. The global COVID-19 pandemic has highlighted the inadequacies within healthcare systems worldwide. Additionally, the availability of quality food has been compromised by the prevalence of packaged and processed foods. The unchecked supply of packaged food materials can lead to compromises in quality, often in the pursuit of cost reduction beyond a reasonable threshold. Similar challenges can be observed in sectors such as cosmetics, where counterfeit products dominate rural markets. A strong ecosystem needs to be established using corporate tax revenue as a foundation, where substandard products become a punishable offence, while high-quality goods receive long-term public support. India, with its substantial market and self-sufficiency in raw materials, is fully capable of creating a national perspective that aligns with long-term growth objectives.

The Indian economic landscape is currently not shaped by the collective needs of the nation or its citizens. Rather, it remains influenced by the strategies of political parties and their pursuit of specific voter groups. This often leads to the manipulation of emotions and individual perspectives for political gains. Unfortunately, these tactics serve the interests of political parties and a select few individuals rather than the entire nation.

However, India possesses the potential to establish a self-sustaining economy that caters to the needs of all sectors, including corporations, politicians, and individuals. Over time, our focus has shifted away from vital areas such as agriculture, manufacturing, innovation, and infrastructure development. Instead, there has been an increasing emphasis on reservations, free entitlements, and short-term individual benefits since gaining independence. These shifts have periodically impacted our economy negatively.

After independence, our initial trajectory included a focus on agriculture, significant corporate growth, and research advancements. Regrettably, we veered off course towards vote-driven politics rather than continued development. In recent times, there has been a renewed emphasis on manufacturing, infrastructure, innovation, and financial services. However, some regions are still behind in terms of agricultural progress and regional development.

The path forward requires us to transcend political divisions and personal interests. Collaboration is essential to boosting every sector and propelling the nation's progress. This entails working diligently in all directions to rejuvenate our economy while placing national interests ahead of political considerations. Our nation is blessed with abundant resources, and we are fully capable of becoming a global economic leader. All it takes is aligning the perspectives of various political parties towards a shared vision of unified development—a singular goal for one nation and one India.

In conclusion, it is vital for governments to address the genuine needs of citizens by prioritising health and education, promoting comprehensive infrastructure development, and fostering an inclusive society. This approach should also involve stringent quality control measures, ensuring that products and services, particularly in the realm of health, food, and cosmetics, meet high standards. By aligning with a unified national perspective, India can harness its economic potential and ensure sustainable growth.

India has a rich history and heritage of cultural accomplishments, innovations, profound ideas, and valuable case studies. It's vital that we recognise this legacy and collectively shape a unified Indian perspective.

This perspective should be centred on achieving the ambitious goal of utilising our abundant resources to become the world's leading economy in diverse sectors including agriculture, innovation, manufacturing, services, and finance.

By drawing inspiration from our history and leveraging the strengths of our people, India can reclaim its status as a global leader. Creating a cohesive and shared vision that transcends regional, political, and individual differences is crucial to steering our nation towards unparalleled growth and development. This entails nurturing our cultural and innovative heritage while directing it towards modern challenges and opportunities.

With a 'one India' perspective, we can harness the strengths of every sector and every individual to collectively drive the nation's progress. By aligning our efforts, we can realise the vision of India not only regaining its historical glory but also becoming a true powerhouse in the world economy across various domains.

6. PERSPECTIVE BASED ON SKILL SET

Skills are not softwares, and the human body is not a machine capable of learning all existing skills. We are a country full of intellectuals with great skills, and those individuals provide direction to the world. Successful individuals should bear the responsibility of guiding society. They must grasp a harsh reality about life—that they have a span of 60 years in which to offer their best, as what comes before and after remains unknown.

Relying solely on the perspective of achieving targets quickly without understanding our core skills is futile. The current generation is only interested insecuring higher returns or pay packages; all other parameters are considered secondary. Many are rushing in one direction—to fulfil personal desires—without contemplating the necessity of their pursuits. In essence, most individuals, whether affluent or not, are part of a rat race. This is true of the entire population. This is why we see most sports aspirants wanting to be cricketers, cricketers wanting to be actors, actors wanting to be leaders, leaders becoming business people or vice versa, and political parties being made up of their leaders' family members. How can we expect quality output from people who have no skills related to the fields they work in?

The same thing applies to Indian corporate families. I am not opposed to the ownership of corporations by families, but running the corporation for sustainable growth requires the right skill set. We need to always think of the nation's growth, corporate growth, and employee growth in relation to our own individual growth. This alignment is only possible when the right skill set is applied at the right time and the right position. Corporate families that dedicate their lives to establishing world-class organisations contribute significantly to job opportunities, growth, and economic development over their 60-year lifespan. Learning life skills within this limited timeframe is crucial, emphasising doing what one's heart beats for.

Unfortunately, many corporate families end up pushing the next generation into the same business without considering their interests or skill sets. While some may enjoy it, others may find themselves making money in ways that are not aligned with their interests. It is crucial for individuals to explore their interests and skills, avoiding a mechanical pursuit of wealth without analysing their own desires.

Life offers two major types of opportunities worldwide: sticking with a single type of task or skill set for a long time or being mismatched and in the wrong place. The key to success is adapting to the right field overtime. However, the number of opportunities to do so is based on luck. The solution to the problem lies in coming out of the box, reflecting, and adapting quickly until we reach the right place with our skills. We should not be swayed by family or peer pressure; no one will else will live life for us. We must embracing failure as a method of learning, fail fast to learn fast, and align our objectives with our skills and interests to reach the right place at the right time.

With each new generation come changes; the ways of the older generation are abandoned. The members of the new generation are not interested in acquiring possessions like flats, cars, and houses. Instead, they seek paths that offer achievement with minimal effort or the possibility of higher rewards through slightly increased effort. They value the concept of smart work over hard work. This trend has both advantages and disadvantages. On the positive side, it helps them avoid falling into traditional traps. However, on the negative side, it means that they might miss out on the ultimate life skill of finding joy in effort. Choosing the easier path may seem appealing, but it's important to strike a balance. While it's great not to be tied to conventional norms, it's also crucial not to overlook the timeless satisfaction that comes from working diligently for one's passions.

Life's value lies in achieving true satisfaction and joy, which cannot solely be measured by money or material growth. Understanding one's intrinsic strengths and working in alignment with them enhances satisfaction, leading to organic financial and personal growth.

In Vedic times, our approach was guided by an inner voice informed by knowledge and shaped by skills. Intuitive and experiential approaches were prevalent, such as accurately describing an elephant's body parts with closed eyes based on sensory experience. In contemporary software development, a similar process unfolds, reflecting unique perspectives and skills. The act of copying and imitating others can potentially divert us from our inner strengths. We must recognise the dynamic nature of progress, take a balanced view oftradition, and embrace new skills.

Interestingly, in contemporary software development, a similar process unfolds. We receive requirements and proceed to define the elephant's body parts, metaphorically speaking, based on our own logical deductions. In software development, diverse developers can generate distinct codes for the same requirement, reflecting their unique perspectives. This proficiency has been deeply ingrained in us across generations. The impulse to imitate and adhere to external principles, procedures, processes, and disciplines as theoretical constructs can sometimes lead us astray. It is essential to recognise that these constructs are by-products of our innate capacity to craft life's logic and naturally deliver outcomes. Copying and imitating others' principles can potentially divert us from the essence of our inner strengths. Our inner wisdom and aptitude for developing life's logic and delivering results should remain at the forefront, enabling us to naturally navigate our paths. This harmonises the principles of both Vedic times and contemporary software development, where authentic intuition and experience contribute significantly.

The foundation of any logic or perspective is a blend of skill sets and ideas. In the Vedic era, we reached a level of mastery in logic, developing numerous theories related to our surroundings, health, the planetary system, science, mathematics, and more. During this time, our logical thinking was highly advanced, reflecting a mature stage of intellectual development. However, as society evolved, we shifted away from this kind of mature logical thinking to a more guided approach. This transition occurred because we struggled to present a unified thought process in the face of an emerging and diverse society. There have been instances when we faced challenges, either as individuals, communities, or as an entire society, particularly when trying to adopt entirely new, mismatched skills.

The transformation from a sophisticated logical approach to a more fragmented one is a part of our historical journey. While we sometimes encounter failures when integrating completely new skills, these experiences are crucial to our evolution. They are reminders of the dynamic nature of progress and adaptation. As we strive to blend the strengths of our history with the innovations of the present, we navigate the delicate balance between preserving tradition and embracing new skills.

I'd like to share a remarkable case study that illustrates the power of skillsets from my perspective. When Mahatma Gandhi returned to India from Africa, many wealthy and established social workers of that time were sceptical about his ability to achieve anything significant in India, as he had done in Africa. They did not believe that Gandhi's methodological and philosophical choices, like not wearing clothes, practising honesty and non-violence, and engaging in menial tasks like serving tea or washing utensils, would address India's problems. These social workers proposed that Gandhi's Africa success be considered a case study for India because his process may not work in India. However, what followed was a remarkable turn of events. Gandhi's logic, ideas, and unique skill set spurred massive, unprecedented mass movements. These movements, including the Salt March, satyagraha, the 'do or die' call, and the Quit India Movement, united Indians across the nation and played a pivotal role in India's struggle for freedom and independence.

This case study underscores Gandhi's distinctive approach to achieving his goal. His methods couldn't be simply transferred through theoretical instruction; they were rooted in practical application and personal conviction. The mass movements that ultimately contributed to India's independence were a direct result of Gandhi's logic and skill set. This highlights the fact that every individual possesses unique skills, perspectives, and approaches. To harness these effectively, it's crucial to recognise and appreciate these differences and channel them in the right direction. Just as Gandhi's approach was distinct and transformative, so too can each individual's skills be harnessed for positive change.

Identifying and harnessing skill sets at the individual, societal, and environmental levels is a crucial step in shaping a comprehensive national perspective. By aligning these skill sets with our growth objectives and desired outcomes, we can effectively guide our progress and development. Furthermore, it's essential to create a global perspective that presents our products and skills to the world. India's historical prowess in agriculture, for instance, positions us well to tap into the growing demand for organic and packaged food products. Leveraging our abundant production of organic grains to create high-quality, ready-to-consume food items is one way our societal skills can be transformed into economic opportunities. Similarly, our strong capabilities in software development highlight the potential of our individual skill sets. Our deep connection with nature can drive initiatives that emphasise sustainability and environmental conservation.

Overall, our perspective underscores the importance of recognising and channelling our unique skill sets at all levels and creating strategies that align with our strengths. This holistic approach can help India attain both domestic and international success while fostering sustainable growth.

7. BREAK THE RULE TO MAKE A NEW ONE

Breaking the rules is not synonymous with defying traditions or laws; rather, it represents a novel approach to learning. To foster fresh and vibrant ideas that can enhance existing rules and benefit humanity, the environment, and society, we must think differently. Innovation necessitates a deep understanding of past failures, which is why text books meticulously detail failed innovations, rules, principles, and theorems. While old rules may seem complex and require more effort to comprehend, new rules are often simpler and more widely accepted, leading to the replacement of the outdated ones. Breaking thought patterns during innovationin the realm of ideas, products, software, and services is essential in all contexts, environments, and societies.

Our thoughts, when pushed to the extreme, can break old rules and pave the way for new innovations. By challenging the boundaries of our thinking, we can move beyond traditional frameworks and spark the birth of new rules and concepts. This process of boundary-pushing and rule-breaking fuels innovation, driving progress across various domains. According to human behaviour principles, innovation often stems from errors or distorted facts, igniting a corrective journey towards the next level of usage. The challenge is to hold onto corrections for long-term perspectives and innovate for the benefit of society, the environment, and the individual.

Initially, we must comprehend our inner strengths. We must carefully work on these strengths, challenging them and seeking feedback from others to refine them. Utilising our inner strengths develops a skill set that requires continuous enhancement through various techniques. Unbiased feedback from a third party, free from interference, is crucial for improvement, considering that a person's perspective is a concealed parameter that can only be understood and altered by human intelligence.

Hence, for unbiased feedback, it's necessary to scrutinise the intricate details of the feedback provider. Even minor shifts in their natural behaviour or environment during feedback can influence or distort the feedback due to a shift in perspective.

Design thinking involves crafting prototypes, testing outcomes, products, and skill sets without revealing one's identity or work, consolidating the results, and evaluating them for a starting point. Once confident in your skill set, breaking rules within that area gradually to formulate new ones, becomes essential. Innovation demands numerous experiments, and these experiments necessitate test cases, requiring a certain level of vulnerability. Applying the design thinking principle to validate oneself through third-party assessment, rather than coercing adaptation. Breaking existing rules is advisable only when you are a master in your field, as seen in physics or science, where adopting new rules involves building upon failed established rules through logical steps and procedures. The sustainability of products, innovations, and services hinges on how effectively we reach the threshold and determine the threshold for innovating new products. If we think we can innovate by merely following linear steps, we're mistaken. Constantly challenging ourselves to align our goals with actual social needs is essential. Vulnerability is beneficial for growth, but quality matters. Vulnerability is particularly effective in areas that you've already mastered, as opposed to skills that are borrowed or imitated. For instance, in sports, experimenting with techniques can pave the way for innovating new techniques. Merely switching fields isn't a feasible solution unless it's a natural progression. All innovations, theories, and principles are developed by building upon the failures of previous innovations, theories, and principles. This progression occurs through logical steps, moving from the recognition of failure to the eventual attainment of success. In this way, the process of innovation is intrinsically tied to the iterative evolution of ideas and concepts, where lessons learnt from past failures lead to the creation of more robust and effective solutions.

Feedback on a finished product or an accurate situation is challenging to obtain. Observable issues with a product or situation create opportunities for feedback, and this is where the mantra 'break the rule to make new one' comes into play. It emphasises the need to understand old rules or possess in-depth knowledge of products and situations to innovate new ones. All innovations, theories, and principles are developed by building upon the failures of previous ones, and this progression occurs through logical steps.

Disregarding others' perspectives in today's era of social media and search engines can be attributed to a lack of awareness. In the age of readily available information, it takes no effort to create your own viewpoint without fully understanding the problem. Relying on search engines or social media hampers innovation, limiting genuine feedback and understanding. It's crucial to map perspectives around us and align our viewpoint appropriately for ourselves and society.

Disregarding others' perspectives in today's era of social media and search engines can be attributed to a lack of awareness. In the age of readily available information, creating your own viewpoint takes no effort. Human psychology often opts for the easiest path—finding solutions without fully understanding the problem and replicating others' perspectives. Formulating your own standpoint based solely on accessible free information, without a genuine comprehension of the actual issue or need, leads to your becoming a product of others' influence and acting accordingly.

I would like to reference a quote by Mr. Pankaj Tripathi, the Bollywood actor, about social media: 'We all are unpaid workers of social media platforms.' He explained this by pointing out the lack of control over people, situations, and ideas. On social media, everything is forwarded, borrowed from others as information, without considering the context or verifying the accuracy of the provided information.

Relying on search engines or social media hampers innovation, as it limits genuine feedback and understanding. It's bound to fail, since authentic feedback isn't obtained. Merely adopting others' perspectives leads us astray from our actual requirements and traps us in viewpoints not truly our own. This emphasises the significance of mapping the perspectives around us and aligning our viewpoint appropriately, whether for ourselves, society, or within a corporate setting. The reason raw perspective-mapping is essential is that we can't change how others view things, and this diversity of perspectives often contributes to confusion in human interactions, societal dynamics, and environmental contexts. Each individual possesses a unique perspective, influenced by various factors like data, information, social media, or social influencers. Given this backdrop, it's crucial to pause, carefully evaluate steps, and cultivate the correct perspective to make informed decisions regarding what's right and wrong. The steps of decision-making are as follows:

1. Maintain all the information and present the true social status separately.

2. Map the genuine need or problem statement that requires resolution.

3. Validate the identified need by seeking direct, one-on-one answers from others. Utilise design thinking or develop a comprehensive raw questionnaire.

4. Analyse and compare all the gathered data points to extract meaningful insights.

5. Align the insights with individual, social, and environmental statuses, considering both short-term and long-term impacts.

6. Develop a long-term perspective based on the acquired insights.

7. Proceed with the decision-making process, incorporating the comprehensive perspective gained through the previous steps.

Creating a perspective on the talk of the town and bigger news eventsand topics like the Ukraine and Russia war or COVID-19 is easy, as you have multiple ready references everywhere. But mapping or creating a perspective for innovation or smaller issues requires multiple steps, multiple case studies, multiple experiments, and multiple failures. Remember, all innovations and new rules emerge from old rules and perspectives that failed.

Achieving 100% accuracy in innovation is beyond our reach, as that power still resides with supernatural forces. Our focus should be on crafting long-term, sustainable products and services that bring positive impacts to people's lives. Rather than adhering to conventional problem-solving methods, we should employ the traditional approach to deeply understand the problem, deviating from the traditional path when innovating new products and services.

Technology follows the lead of human ingenuity, as the human brain possesses more cells than any machine. As of now, no technology can surpass human intelligence. Thus, our approach should involve physical interaction to understand the problem and the product requirements of humans, society, and the environment. The subsequent steps involve development, developing the product through various stages of its lifecycle, generating common product data points to create machine learning models, and eventually fashioning AI models from multiple patterns of machine learning. These AI models naturally evolve to consistently produce accurate results, becoming a part of human nature. This holistic cycle represents the continuous process of generating new rules by breaking the old ones—the journey of innovation.

If our aspiration is not to remain stagnant but to evolve, we must redefine ourselves and establish fresh targets, even if that entails significant changes. Every perspective involves gradual steps and learning from experience. As we achieve success, it's vital to incorporate additional steps into our path to success. Remarkable accomplishments often emerge effortlessly only after numerous attempts marked by failures and lessons learnt. The oscillation between great times and tough times, lows and highs, failures and successes, is inherent to life and represents two sides of the same coin. And life changes based on one's perspective on life and related practices.

The experience of navigating the challenges posed by COVID-19 has fortified us, and this resilience will translate into creating favourable circumstances for our survival. Favourable times give rise to a complacent citizenry, which, in turn, can lead to a decline in inner strength due to a lack of effort. This cyclical pattern of evolution continues unless interrupted. Our task is to break this cycle and cultivate the ability to consistently generate great times, remarkable products, positive environments, and flourishing societies. This requires a continuous commitment to growth and improvement.

In this era, breaking away from the norm is remarkably achievable. We can step out of the realm of social media technology, and internet information, and return to the simple act of interacting with people as genuine human beings. By doing so, we naturally venture out of conventional and into uncharted territory. This shift in perspective allows us to challenge established norms, dismantle existing rules, and envision novel societal needs. Within the confines of larger global corporations, there's a risk of losing touch with the fundamental aspects of life—essentials like clean air and water, life skills, and genuine human interaction. It's time to disconnect from these traps and embark on a journey to restore these core aspects of human existence. By disconnecting from the noise and distractions, we can rediscover and rectify the basics that contribute to a wholesome and fulfilling human life.

I want to rest my case here.

Taking action is essential for our survival, personal growth, and making the most of the limited time we have on this planet. Every second of our life is indeed precious, and while we can't control everything, we can certainly control how we choose to live and make the most of each moment.

Thanks for reading, but remember, continuous action is needed to survive billions of years as human, 100s of years as a single known life and eternal happiness every second of our life as it is precious and uncontrollable. Don't waste time, and don't wait for things to happen—take charge, seize opportunities, and work towards your goals to create a fulfilling and purposeful life.